This Book Belongs To:

Aladdin
and the
Magic Lamp

Illustrated by
Greg Hildebrandt
Retold from
The Thousand and One Nights

The Unicorn Publishing House, Inc.
New Jersey

Aladdin
and the
Magic Lamp

here was once a boy named Aladdin. And, in truth, he was a very lazy boy. Instead of minding his mother and helping with the chores, Aladdin would run off to play in the streets.

Aladdin only came home for his meals and never once did he offer to help his poor mother. His father had died some years back, and so his mother had to weave yarn all day long to support herself and her son.

But all that changed when an evil wizard came calling one evening at the door.

Aladdin and the Magic Lamp

The evil wizard pretended to be Aladdin's uncle, and gave beautiful presents to the boy and his mother. He wept bitterly when the mother told of her husband's death.

"Oh! what sorrow!" cried the clever wizard. "I have been gone these forty years far to the west, and now I have come home to find my dear brother is dead! If only I had known!"

The wizard pulled at his hair and cried so terribly that Aladdin and his mother were soon convinced that he was indeed the boy's uncle.

"I must make amends for my absence. Please, let me help you and your son. I am rich and would gladly help the boy become a man."

The mother thanked him with tears of joy.

Aladdin and the Magic Lamp

The wizard came early the next morning. He greeted Aladdin warmly and took him for a pleasant walk. But the walk began to grow very long. And before Aladdin knew it, he was in a deep dark valley. He begged the wizard to stop.

"We shall go no farther," replied the wizard. "Now go and gather dry sticks for a fire." And when the fire was made, the wizard began to chant strange words and the ground opened wide, revealing a stone door with a great brass ring.

Aladdin would have run from fright, but the wizard grabbed him and said: "You, my boy, shall be rich! Only you can open this door and gain the treasure inside. The stars have foretold it. Inside are great riches, but touch nothing until you have taken the lamp at the end of the cave. Then you can gather the other treasure. Wear this ring, my boy, and it will protect you when all else fails. Now go!"

And Aladdin did as he was told.

Aladdin and the Magic Lamp

Once inside the cave, Aladdin wasted no time in finding the lamp. He quickly tied the lamp to his belt and started back.

It was then that Aladdin noticed the riches around him. But he was very fearful of the cave. He only stopped once to gaze at two beautiful trees full of the most wonderful fruits. Looking closer, he saw the fruits were really stones. Aladdin believed the stones to be glass, but he thought them pretty and picked as many as he could carry away.

The weight of the stones made it hard to get back out. Aladdin called out: "Uncle, please, I cannot reach the door without your help."

"Fine, my boy, I will help you. But first, hand me up the lamp. Quickly now," the wizard demanded.

"I cannot reach it, uncle," Aladdin pleaded. "If only you would help me out, then I can give you the lamp."

Aladdin and the Magic Lamp

The wizard thought the boy was trying to cheat him. He became furious, and said: "If I cannot have the lamp, then no one shall!" In the next moment, the cave door shut and Aladdin was trapped.

For three days poor Aladdin sat sobbing in the cave, until at last he felt death was near. He fell to his knees and clasped his hands in prayer. And as he joined his hands, he rubbed the ring the wizard had given him. In a flash of light and smoke, an enormous genie appeared, saying: "I am the Genie of the Ring. Command me and I shall obey."

Though terribly frightened, Aladdin cried out: "Oh, please genie, take me from this place and return me home."

No sooner were the words spoken than his wish was granted. He found himself just outside his house.

Aladdin and the Magic Lamp

Aladdin told his mother of the wizard's betrayal, and how the magic genie had saved him. Then he showed her the strange lamp.

"Heaven be thanked, you are safe," said the mother; "but you must have something to eat. Let me clean this lamp and sell it at market for some food." Aladdin happily agreed.

She took the lamp outside to polish it. She had scarcely begun to rub the lamp, when there arose a great genie even larger than the first. The genie spoke with a voice like thunder, saying: "I am the Genie of the Lamp. What do you wish? Command me and I shall obey."

Aladdin's mother was too terrified to speak, but Aladdin, who had seen a genie in the cave, seized the lamp, and answered firmly: "I am hungry. Bring food that I may eat."

Aladdin and the Magic Lamp

The genie disappeared, and returned in a moment carrying a large silver tray on which were twelve silver dishes filled with the finest food. There were also silver pitchers filled with good wine and bowls of ripe, sweet fruit.

The kingly feast lasted several days. When the food was gone, Aladdin went to market and sold the silver dishes. A change had come over Aladdin, who no longer ran about the streets, but stayed at home. Aladdin was becoming a man.

When Aladdin went to market to sell the silver tray, he decided to show the jeweller one of the curious stones he had plucked from the trees in the cave.

"Tell me, sir, do you think this of any value?" Aladdin asked, still believing the stone was simply colored glass.

Aladdin and the Magic Lamp

The jeweller took the stone in his trembling hands.

"I...I have never seen a ruby as large as this!" he gasped. "Why, it's worth a king's ransom, and more!"

Aladdin was stunned to find he was rich. Why, he had a whole basketful of these stones! But Aladdin was content with the money for the silver tray. After all, his mother and he really didn't need all that much. He was content, yes, or so he thought.

On his way home, Aladdin stopped to admire the sultan's grand palace. Curious to see how the rich passed their days, he climbed a large tree outside the wall of the palace gardens—just to have a peek.

Once there, Aladdin's eyes rested upon the most beautiful thing he had ever beheld—the lovely face of the princess. Aladdin's heart swelled with love for her.

Aladdin and the Magic Lamp

Aladdin told his mother that evening of his love for the princess. He begged his mother to take the jewels and offer them to the sultan for his daughter's hand in marriage.

His mother agreed, and went to the palace the very next morning. She waited all day to see the sultan. When she came before him at last, she fell upon her knees and begged: "Mercy for me and my son, great sultan. He bid me to come before you and ask your daughter's hand in marriage for his sake. He hopes you will accept this gift as proof of his love for the princess." And she spread the jewels out before him.

For several moments he said nothing. Then he cried: "They are so beautiful. So...so rich! Rise, rise, good woman! Go back and tell your son he shall have my daughter in marriage, but he must wait three months to the day before the wedding takes place."

Aladdin and the Magic Lamp

Aladdin cried with joy at hearing the happy news. He readily agreed to wait three months.

But when three months had passed, Aladdin found he was betrayed. Instead of his wedding taking place, the princess was wed to the son of the sultan's chief advisor.

"The princess was promised to me, and though she knows not of my love now, she soon will!" And he rubbed the lamp, calling to the genie: "I command you to go to the sultan's palace this night, and every night, and bring the princess to my home. Take her new husband and leave him out in the cold, returning them both to the palace each morning unharmed."

The genie obeyed. He brought the princess every night to Aladdin's home and carried the poor husband outside the palace walls, leaving him to shiver in the cold. "Fear not, princess," Aladdin would say, "no harm will come to you." Then he would lie down beside her bed and go to sleep.

Aladdin and the Magic Lamp

No one believed the couple when they told what happened. After a week, the husband begged the sultan to dissolve the marriage, saying he simply couldn't take anymore.

When Aladdin heard that the marriage was over, he rubbed the lamp, and the genie appeared, saying: "What is your wish, O master? Command me and I shall obey."

Aladdin spoke: "I wish for forty servants, each carrying a large bowl full of gold and upon each head a tray full of fine pearls and precious stones. Send them to the sultan and present the treasure as my gift." When this was done, Aladdin made straight away for the palace.

Aladdin entered the palace and demanded the sultan keep his promise of marriage. When the sultan beheld the riches given by Aladdin, he happily agreed. Amid great joy, Aladdin and the princess were wed. Aladdin then called upon the genie to build him the grandest palace in all the world. By the very next morning, the palace was finished.

Aladdin and the Magic Lamp

Aladdin and the princess moved into the great palace, and began their happy life together. And a happy life it would have remained—but for one thing.

"No! No! No!" cried the evil wizard. "The wretched boy lives? And my lamp, my precious lamp, for his pleasure? Thief! Well, young Aladdin, your good fortune will soon come to an end, my boy. I will see to that! The lamp and the princess will be mine! Mine!"

The wizard laughed a vile laugh and gazed deeper into the black pool. From there the wizard could conjure up the images of Aladdin, the princess, the great palace—the lamp. When he thought he had seen enough, the wizard left his dark palace and journeyed to Aladdin's home.

Aladdin and the Magic Lamp

"Old lamps for new! Old lamps for new!" came a cry from the street below the palace. Aladdin was away on business, but the princess heard the odd cry and looked out the palace window. She saw a raggedy old man, calling: "Who will exchange old lamps for new?"

Now Aladdin had not revealed where the genie came from. So when the princess heard the call for old lamps, she picked up Aladdin's lamp and hurried down to the street.

"Here, good sir, I have an old lamp to trade for a new one," said the princess. "Ah, dear princess," said the wizard sweetly, "you do me a great honor. Here you are, my princess, a brand new lamp for this old one."

The princess gave the wizard Aladdin's lamp and took the new one. Delighted, she returned to the palace. Aladdin will be so pleased when he returns, the princess thought.

Aladdin and the Magic Lamp

"Ha, ha! Silly, silly child!" laughed the wizard, rubbing the lamp with glee. The genie appeared, saying: "I am the Genie of the Lamp. Command me and I shall obey."

"Excellent! Excellent! I wish for this palace and the princess within to be taken with me to my land far to the west. At once I say!" And in a blink of an eye, they were gone.

Aladdin returned that day to find his wife and his home had vanished. For three long days Aladdin searched the desert. All in vain. At last he knelt down to pray. At that moment he remembered the ring. Rubbing the ring, the genie appeared. "I am the Genie of the Ring. Command me and I shall obey." Aladdin jumped up, shouting: "Return to me my princess and my palace!"

"I cannot master, for only the Genie of the Lamp has such power, but I can take you there." The next moment the genie was flying Aladdin far above the earth, till at last Aladdin caught sight of the palace.

Aladdin and the Magic Lamp

The genie set Aladdin down just outside the palace. He handed him a small bottle, saying: "Take this potion, master, and find a way for the wizard to drink it. Beware! his evil magic is strong. Only this charm will stop him."

Aladdin climbed through the bedroom window and found his beloved princess. "Aladdin, my love, I knew you would come!" she cried. But Aladdin begged her to be silent, and gave her the magic potion. "Hurry, or all will be lost!"

"Ah, my dear!" the wizard said. "Have you at last come to your senses and forgotten that good-for-nothing boy?"

"Yes, my lord, I have. I only needed a little time," replied the princess sweetly. "My lord, let us drink a toast to our new life together." She poured the wizard a glass of wine and slipped the potion inside. The wizard drank deep.

"No! No! you wicked child!" screamed the wizard, clutching at his throat. In an instant, the genie appeared, saying: "I am the Genie of the Lamp, and I have COME for you."

Aladdin and the Magic Lamp

The genie rose up and grabbed the wizard. Then he dragged him, kicking and screaming, back inside the lamp. There it is said, he is to be enslaved forevermore.

With the wizard gone, Aladdin took the lamp in his hands and rubbed it. "I am the Genie of the Lamp. What do you wish, master? Command me and I shall obey always."

"I wish for you to fly us home, genie," Aladdin said, then looking at his princess, he softly repeated: "Home."

"Your wish is my command, master."

And home they went.

This book is dedicated
to my daughter,
Mary,
because she makes me laugh.

Greg Hildebrand